Yuletide Invasion

Terror At The Dance

J.C. Moore

MISSING STAR BOOKS

Also By

Soured: A Collection Of Short Stories (Dark Intrigues Book 1)

Tainted: A Collection Of Short Stories (Dark Intrigues Book 2)

Yuletide Invasion: A Holiday Horror Novella

The Repayment

Copyright ©2023 by J.C. Moore

All rights reserved.

No portion of this book may be reproduced in any form without written permission from the publisher or author except as permitted by U.S. copyright law. This is a work of fiction. Names, characters, places, and incidents either are the product of the author's imagination or are used fictitiously. Any resemblance to actual persons, living or dead, events, or locales is entirely coincidental.

Edited by Christine Morgan

Cover Design–Jorge Iracheta

Cover Wrap - J.C. Moore

Interior Art - Metamoraki

ISBN: 9798865013815

WARNING: This book contains scenes and subject matter that are disturbing, gory, and possibly offensive.

FOR SIGNED BOOKS, MERCHANDISE, AND EXCLUSIVE ITEMS VISIT: WWW.JCMOOREAUTHOR.COM

Contents

Introduction	1
Prologue	4
The Crash	7
Christmas Wonderland	18
Hanging The Tinsel	25
Matt's Lie	29
The Dance	35
Gloria's Past	46
The Thing In Carla	54
The Hatching	62
Feed Us	76

A Run For Survival	81
Making A Stand	86
The Others Arrive	91
Emily's Face	98
Acknowledgements	103
Thank You	105
Get Free Stories	106
About the Author	107

To Joe, Tom, Vince, Russ, and Brian - my friends.

**And what was in those ships all three,
On Christmas day, on Christmas day?
And what was in those ships all three,
On Christmas day in the morning?**

—William Sandys

"I Saw Three Ships"

Introduction

As I complete this year's sequel to "Yuletide Invasion," I'm caught in a unique blend of holiday joy. A small, unassuming plastic Santa Claus sits sentinel on my cluttered desk, casting a spectral, painted-on smile. The room resonates with twinkling lights and taunting carols.

Halloween's spooky embrace looms just around the corner, a time when I should cavort with my beloved entourage of macabre confidantes—skeletons, monstrous amalgamations, and other denizens of the supernatural underworld. But such, my friends, is the peculiar existence of a writer.

So, are you prepared for a wild, eldritch ride through the darkest depths of Christmas horrors? I hope so, as once again I offer an antidote to the usual Lifetime Holiday rom-com, the same old Scrooge story and Santa's insane rampages.

I'm determined to recreate the nostalgic feel of past cinematic and literary masterpieces once more.

Imagine yourself in the eerie '50s, where *"Creature from the Black Lagoon"* (1954) evoked fear with its aquatic horrors lurking beneath the surface. Or fast forward to the neon-soaked '80s, a time when *"Ghoulies"* (1985) crawled out of the darkest corners, where evil creatures from another world descended upon hapless victims, echoing the horrors that infuse the very essence of *"Yuletide Invasion."*

"Evil Dead" (1981) carved its niche with its relentless onslaught of the supernatural, a feeling of relentless terror that I aspire to evoke within these pages. The otherworldly menace of *"Alien"* (1979), where a silent, deadly predator lurked in the cold, unfeeling void of space, has also been an ever-present inspiration.

And let's not forget *"The Shining"* (1980), where the Overlook Hotel served as a breeding ground for hostility, blurring the lines between madness and the supernatural, all while trapped by an innocent blanket of snow.

Classics like *"Evil Eye"* by Ehren M. Ehly (1989) have left their indelible mark in my book world, showcasing how a book can delve into the darkest recesses of human fear. *"The House of Thunder"* by Dean Koontz (1982) masterfully wove a narrative of unrelenting suspense and supernatural intrigue.

And, of course, the late and great Richard Laymon, with his unique ability to craft tales that push the boundaries of human terror. His legacy flows through my latest holiday havoc story.

So, dear readers, brace yourselves for a journey that marries the classic chillers of the past with a modern twist, where the ordinary transmutes into the extraordinary, and the mundane becomes macabre.

Prepare yourself - it will be absolute lunacy!

J.C.

October, 2023

Prologue

AS IF IT WERE a gift from Hell, a blizzard swept through Elview, New York, on Christmas Eve in 1986. A terror beyond human imagination hit the unsuspecting hamlet as snowflakes cascaded from the sky.

Horrific figures emerged, seething with bloodlust. But a handful of brave souls stood their ground, refusing to concede.

This year, Elview is once again cold and dreary. As the town prepares for the annual Christmas Dance, their merriment only distracts from the wicked secrets that are now stirring in the shadows of their minds. Few speak of what they saw — of those dark things that crept from beyond time and space — and more have ignored it, believing it was nothing more than a ghostly figment of their imagination.

Now, approach this blazing fire closer. I was hoping you could sit beside me and gaze deeply into the flames, for I have a most strange and thrilling tale to share with you. As the licking tongues of flame dance wildly, close your eyes and let me take you through a harrowing story born of shadows and mysteries from beyond.

This Yuletide promises a journey into an abyss of horror.

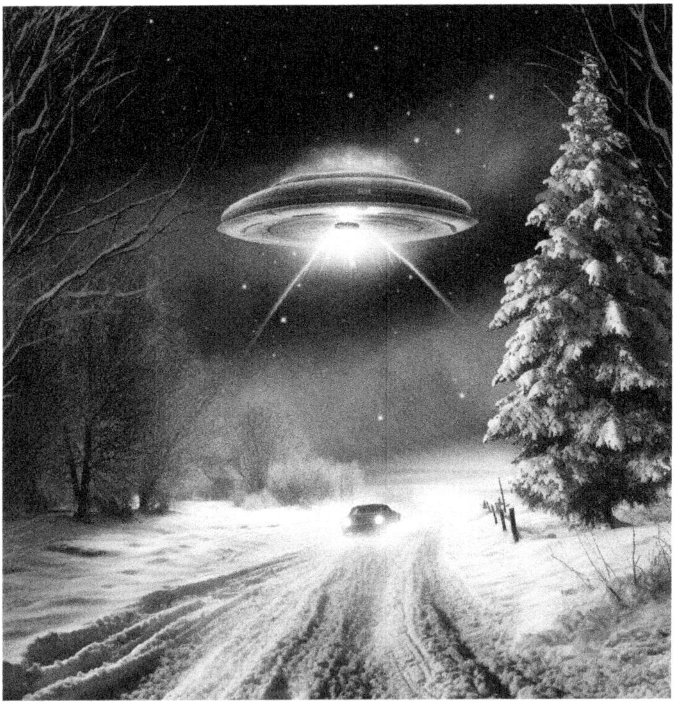

The Crash

December 23, 2023

A BOVE THE BACK SEAT of his ancient Chevy, Frank hung mistletoe as the snowstorm raged. Curious, he peered into the storm. Then he averted his gaze and skillfully rolled up a joint before swiftly chugging from a bottle of whiskey. Watching in awe, Carla's eyes sparkled with a radiance that conveyed her comfort with his enjoyment of risk.

Frank had a face of darkness, his wild hair framing it in chaotic disorder, and the wispy patches of beard emphasized his untamed nature. Carla felt something within her awaken; he was no Greek God but an irresistible force she wanted to be taken by.

The night was far from ideal. Carla and Frank had stopped at Pizza & Pasta, a grungy restaurant with flabby toppings and soggy crusts. But it didn't matter to her that Frank was always short on cash — she would take what she could get. Next, they went to The Elviews, an ancient movie theater with the stench of moldering carpets and musty seats. It played a decades-old Christmas horror flick named *Black Christmas*.

As dusk descended, they went to Lover's Lookout. The cops kept a watchful eye but rarely interfered with the occupants of automobiles. Frank switched on some unknown song, desperately attempting to create an ambiance of serenity. However, she quickly changed it to a song from the past — allowing Motley Crue's 'Home Sweet Home' to flood the vehicle.

Frank scrunched his face, recoiling as the raucous melody blared through the speakers.

"I loathe this song," he said, "with every fiber of my being."

She smiled sweetly as she increased the volume, saying, "Well, I love it."

"But it is almost Christmas. How about one of those stupid all-Christmas song stations?"

Carla shook her head vehemently, a cascade of copper curls tumbling across her forehead.

"No frigging way," she said, her upper lip curling in disgust. "Those songs are so lame and overused. Give me some good old-fashioned rock' n' roll any day."

Frank lifted the bottle of whiskey to his lips and took a deep pull, the fiery liquid burning his throat as it went down. He looked at Carla with a devilish glint in his eye, and she couldn't help but laugh despite herself.

"Let's make this night one we'll never forget," he said, the liquor and joint loosening his tongue. He leaned in close, his voice low. "I'm talking about something that will stay with us forever."

He leaned closer, and their noses almost touched. The dashboard lights illuminated their shadows and silhouetted them in an ethereal radiance. His offer was corny, but Carla always gave in.

"You sure know how to sweet-talk a woman," she said playfully, pressing her body closer to his. "But I'm game if you are."

Frank gazed into her eyes, unbuttoning her top, and in a minute, the fabric had cascaded around her waist. He'd chosen her outfit himself—a teal blue shirt and skirt—which now lived in an amorphous pile beside them on the leather car seat. Shivers of pleasure fell over her as she reclined there with a satisfied grin.

A low, hungry whisper escaped Frank's lips.

"This is what I'm talking about."

Carla grasped his neck with a vise-like grip, pressing her lips into his. A snowstorm engulfed them outside the car.

"You're a wild one, Frank," she purred into his ear. "And I love it."

He grinned devilishly as his hands explored her body. She shivered with pleasure, her skin reacting to each touch.

The feeble warmth from the rusty vents couldn't extinguish the flames between Carla and Frank as they kissed. He pounced on her with a savage intensity that made her gasp for air. His eager hands continued exploring her body as he thrust deeper and harder, letting out a low, throaty growl with each movement.

He marveled at Carla's lack of inhibition, as if she were one of those faceless women from the porn he often watched. As their bodies collided with raw ferocity, a sudden bright flare spat into the night sky, a dazzling illumination slicing through the darkness. A loud boom rumbled across the fields, sending snowflakes soaring up like an eruption. The ground rattled beneath them with shuddering force, launching powdery snow as a geyser emerged.

He froze. "What the hell was that?"

A shriek tore from her throat as she dug her nails into his back. "Please, don't stop! Harder!" she wailed, her body wracked by uncontrollable quakes.

But, as she peered out the window, she gasped. A gigantic crater filled the snow-covered fields, with smoke rising from its depths like an angry phoenix. The blue light dazzled her eyes, and a loud buzzing filled her head like a thousand bees. Then there was silence in the car as the radio stopped playing. With a sudden 'POP,' the interior lights blazed on and then exploded, leaving them in darkness with only eerie blue light casting strange shadows around them.

"What the hell?" they said in unison, their mouths agape.

Frank pulled Carla close and felt her shudder beneath his hands.

While searching for clothes, he sensed her fear simmering behind her eyes. He reached for the driver's side door even before he finished zipping up his pants.

"Stay put," he said, not giving her a chance to argue.

"Don't leave me, baby."

"Just wait here. I'll go check out what that is." His voice quivered as he spoke.

"Let's just go, Frank. I don't like this."

A tense silence hung like a tomb as Frank slowly reached for the ignition. He cringed at the expectation of a fruitless attempt, yet he still had to try. His heart raced as his shaking hand turned the key. Yet nothing happened. Not even the faintest sound emerged from under the hood.

Frank squinted through the darkness, his jaw hanging open as he pointed at the swirling lights in mid-air above the smoking crater.

"What in the hell? Look at that!"

Carla's voice wavered as she asked, "Oh my God, what is that?"

"I have no clue, babe."

Suddenly, another geyser burst up, and the lights around the crater flickered out, leaving them bathed in an eerie silence punctuated by a shrill whistling sound. Frank wiped his nose and noticed a small trickle of blood flowing from it.

"Fuck me," he muttered under his breath.

Fear clawed at Carla's throat as she frantically searched for her phone. Like a stark reminder of her sinking hopes, she found the battery was dead. She glanced over at Frank, nearly immobilized by the dread that had consumed her, and saw his eyes glued to the scene.

Frank clawed at his clothes, yanking them on in a manic frenzy. His hands trembled as he laced his boots and threw on his heavy winter coat.

"I know I'm going to regret this," he said as he reached for the door handle. "But I have to see what that is. I can't help it."

"NO!" she shrieked, desperately clinging to his arm. "Please don't leave me here. This can't be a coincidence—the car and our phones dying simultaneously? It's like something out of a horror movie."

He carefully extracted her fingers from his coat sleeve and opened the driver's side door. He emerged into the raging snowstorm, intent on finding some answer.

Frank's breath left him in white plumes against the snow-swept sky as he shuffled forward. His boots waded through icy drifts, immersing him in a frigid sea while sweat slicked his back. He paused at a crater; its borders blackened like charred wood. A massive object jutted from the ground, metallic and smoking, like some hellish creature woken from its slumber beneath the earth.

His heart raced with terror and exhilaration, his feet sinking deep into the snowdrifts. As he approached, he could feel an oppressive heat emanating from the mysterious object and only felt more emboldened to discover what secrets it may contain. A wave of courage washed over him, and Frank wrenched open what looked like a hatch to behold an even vaster anomaly hidden within.

A cold, slimy object emerged from the hatch, piercing Frank's stomach and inflicting excruciating pain. His eyes widened with dread at seeing a monstrous creature before him. It was tall, its body bulging with thick, gray leather-like skin. Its face had an expressionless stare and a gaping maw lined with razor-sharp teeth that opened like a festering wound. Tentacles sprouted from its neck, wrapping around Frank's arms and legs as it lifted him off the ground. He felt their tight grip choking off his breath, pushing down his throat to swallow him whole. Frank fought against the creature, fueling its rage as it tightened its hold on him...but there seemed to be no escape.

Another malformed horror from the depths of nightmares slithered from the smoldering ruins, its saucer eyes burning with unholy fire. A noise escaped its mouth — a soul-searing screech that chilled Frank to his core. Its tentacles writhed and unfurled like a bouquet of evil snaking their way across his body. No amount of pleading could save him from the onslaught of terror he now found himself in; the abomination had him suspended in midair, its brutish grasp pinning him to the spot as it felt and prodded at every inch of his exposed flesh, reveling in his agony.

Frank's fragile mind split like a delicate porcelain doll dropped from a great height as the sinister extra-dimensional beings intensified their intrusive prying. His body quaked with terror, and he lost all control of himself, his fear forcefully expelling its contents in a thick brown stain on the pure snow beneath his feet.

Frank heard Carla's desperate cries, and before the impenetrable darkness crept in, he thought to himself with a fleeting sense of clarity: if only they had stayed in that night instead of going out on their date. A relentless and unknown force soon consumed this realization.

The shapes moved with an otherworldly speed, their echoing clacking resembling that of an army of spiders. As they approached, an audible hum seemed to resonate from them toward the car, causing Carla's head to throb painfully. She screamed desperately, slamming her hands against the car windows to flee.

A horrifying sizzle split the air, followed by an electric snap that released a blinding shower of sparks like a burning firework. A halo of blue energy cast an eerie light across the figures, who ripped off the driver's side door and enveloped her in an icy embrace. She trembled in fear as it caressed her bare skin.

A torrent of terror filled her veins as the tentacled monstrosities lunged into the car. Her screams echoed through the night as she scrambled backward, desperately seeking escape. Clutching the passenger door handle, she plunged into the winter air, thick snowflakes crunching beneath her bare feet. She felt the icy wind slicing across her as she sprinted for her life, pushing herself to new heights of stamina and fear. Then, a force slammed into her from behind, sending her face-first into an abyss of white powder that threatened to swallow her whole.

She spun around in terror, staring in fear at the ghastly figures standing before her. Bathed in a dim light, their skin took on a sickly blue hue. Their round eyes emitted a soft glow. Each of their mouths dripped with writhing tentacles that undulated in the winter storm.

With a blood-curdling scream, she launched herself into the midst of her tormentors. But they were too powerful and soon dragged her back to the snow-covered earth. The glint of a curved blade in the dying light caught her eye as one creature raised a wickedly sharp instrument.

The blade carved its way through her tender flesh, rending apart her abdomen from her throat to her groin. Excruciating pain ripped through every nerve as it dug deep within her body, seeking secrets and ravaging her deepest recesses. Slithering tentacles invaded her being, penetrating each organ and tearing at her private spaces. Everywhere they ventured, there was a deafening silence;

it seemed the winter air had held its breath in anticipation of their exploration. As she shuddered in agony, the frigid embrace brought a numbness that consumed everything around her until only darkness remained.

Christmas Wonderland

Haley Roberts scowled at the lurid decorations of Christmas Wonderland; her face twisted in disgust. Earlier in the day, shoppers had swarmed around her like frenzied ants, their wallets bulging with holiday cheer. The clanging bells and wailing children blended in a cacophony.

The unending stream of purchasers at the checkout terminal had eventually abated. But her hatred towards her occupation only intensified with each clock tick. How could these soulless will-o'-the-wisps not comprehend that the future of retail lived within their very palms?

Elview was a forgotten spot on the map, unassuming and overlooked. The mayor had an idea to take RJ's Super Market & Convenience Store — infamous for its cursed events on Christmas Eve in 1986 — and turn it into a seasonal destination. He hoped it would pull out more than just the locals from the rut of their daily lives. His scheme proved successful; people from Buffalo and its outskirts began trooping to Elview to see the new amusement park-like store.

A deep voice broke her trance. Haley's gaze traveled to the source — Matt, her colleague, bearing a precarious stack of boxes. "Hey, Haley! You alright? You look like you could faint."

She weakly nodded in response. "Yeah, I'm okay. Just tired. No rest for the wicked."

He chuckled nervously, and his gaze flickered around the store as if expecting something to jump out at them. "This holiday shit is killing us all. At least we're not dealing with whatever happened here in '86, right?"

"True that," she said, still feeling uneasy. "But this sucks just as bad; super lame."

"I hear you. Nobody likes work, but at least we are making some money."

"I guess..."

Haley reached for a candy cane by her register, unwrapped it, and popped it into her mouth. The sweet rush worked its way down her throat, helping suppress the fear that had taken root since she had started her shift.

She glanced at Matt, who was now stacking boxes on the shelves behind them, but the dread lingered like a mist.

"It's hard to feel festive when surrounded by all this plastic crap," she said, gazing out across the store.

"Ya, but we still get to work together," he replied. "It could be worse."

"I guess."

Elview's Christmas Wonderland may have looked harmless and cheerful on the outside, but beneath its flashy lights and tinsel, Haley felt something was wrong.

He put his hand on her back. "Come on now, don't be a Grinch. It's Christmas Eve!"

"Oh, joy to the world," she scoffed.

Matt's grin faltered. "Hey, what's wrong? You've been acting weird all day."

Haley hesitated for a moment, then let out a sigh. "This 'holiday season' is a mockery," she hissed, her voice low and venomous. "What was merry has become nothing more than greed and soulless consumption. Just look at this place," She gestured wildly towards the flashy lights and faux snowflakes that littered the area, "Christmas Wonderland! As if any of these displays the true beauty of Christmas." Her tone had sharpened with every word, and she seemed ready to spit fire by the end of her rant.

Matt's eyes widened. "That was a real zinger you just dropped. But, hey, I think you're alright despite it all."

"Sorry, Matt," she said. "I know I'm being a bore. It's hard to feel jolly when everything around us looks like this."

"We just need to hang on for a few more hours. Then we can go home, bury this place in the past, and never look back... never think of it again."

"Oh, yes, please! Let this shitty season be nothing more than a forgotten nightmare." Her Christmas bells mocked her, cruelly adorning the blouse she wished to incinerate.

"Man, though, I'm pumped for the dance tomorrow!" he said. "It's gonna be so wild! Everyone will be there, and I'm going with Riley Hallman. But I feel like I'm about to hurl -—she's way out of my league!"

"You'll do great. You are a cool guy. Anyone would be lucky to go with you."

"Who are you going with?"

"Nobody," Haley answered after a beat, her eyes rolling in exasperation. She slumped onto the cash register counter, crossing her arms firmly and scowling at the floor. "The thought of dancing makes me want to vomit."

"Well," he cut in, staring at the floor. "It would be cool to see you."

"And, celebrations? Ha. Not this year. It's been three years since my dad bit the dust, and I'm still stuck in this empty pit of bullshit. While my mom's out there doing her cop thing. I just wanna sit in my new apartment and eat junk food and watch dumb holiday flicks."

"How is the new apartment?"

She shrugged. "Small. But it'll do its job until I can save enough money to move somewhere bigger. It's not much, but at least it's mine."

"Did you put up the little Christmas tree I gave you?"

Haley nodded slowly, a small smile tugging at the corners of her lips. "Yup, put it up alright. Cute made the hovel feel more like a home." She paused before continuing softly, "Thanks, man. Appreciate it."

"Why don't you and I meet up later? We can catch one of those sappy holiday movies together."

"That sounds... nice," Haley said softly, feeling her heart swell as an unfamiliar spark of hope ignited within her.

A massive, middle-aged woman with startling pink hair gripped a tattered overcoat as she strode to the front of the line. She wore a Santa hat sweatshirt. "Cash me out already. Or are you idiots going to keep on yammerin' away?"

Haley's stomach nearly revolted as 'All I Want for Christmas Is You' by Mariah Carey blared from the speakers like a never-ending nightmare of holiday terror.

"Of course, ma'am," Haley replied with forced politeness.

The woman's voice was a tumult of hostility and scorn, her breath stinking of cheap booze and cigarettes. "Don't you get all high and mighty on me, little lady."

Haley hurriedly finished the transaction and watched as the woman slowly shuffled out of the store into the snowy outside, her raspy mutterings echoing in her wake.

Haley's gaze hardened.

"Ah yes, I'm so relieved to be leaving this place," she declared with a sigh, her mouth drawing a grim line. "This has been like the stuff of nightmares. This is my last shift until after Christmas. Have yourself a great Christmas, Matt. May you have an amazing time at the dance."

Matt asked eagerly, "Get together tomorrow then? I'd love nothing more than to hang with you, Haley."

A sly smirk slowly overtook her face. "You never know," she said, almost tauntingly. "It could be ... fun. Anything might happen."

She hastily buttoned up her winter coat, wrapping it tightly around her body, and spared one last glance at Matt before she flung open the door and charged into the icy winter night.

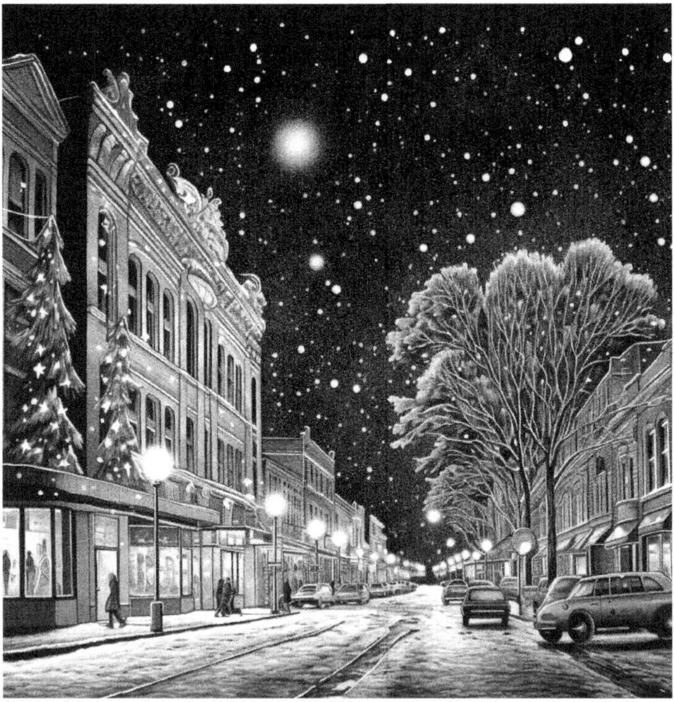

Hanging The Tinsel

Twirling, Chrissie marveled at the lavish decorations for the dance her committee assembled. She had taken the lead; her best friend Denise, a seemingly lifeless form, slumped in a metal folding chair. Perpetual vape clouds surrounded Denise's blond head as her thumbs ceaselessly tapped away on her phone.

"Help me hang this fucking tinsel already!" Chrissie pointed at the tangled mess of metallic strands.

Dean Martin's raspy, drunken voice rang through the room. In response, Denise let out a guttural howl, "It's a marshmallow world!"

"What's got into you, girl?" Chrissie asked. "You normally couldn't give two shits about Christmas."

"Is it wrong for me to have some fun and at least attempt to get into the holiday spirit?" Denise challenged.

The guilt washed over Chrissie as she felt the heat surging through her veins, her teeth grinding to suppress it.

Denise marched around the room like she was still the high school queen — stunning and arrogant, expecting everyone to honor her. But Chrissie stumbled behind her, desperate to keep up. Decades had passed, but they were still two sides of a sharp coin, unable to alter their positions or break away from each other. Even with all their faults and resentments, they still loved one another.

Her breath hitched as she placed another strand of silvery tinsel on the evergreen tree. "Forget it. I'm just being stupid."

Principal Gregory entered the gymnasium, his face a mask of cheerfulness. He scanned the decorations suspiciously, and his eyes locked on Chrissie and Denise, who were now arguing about garlands to the sickeningly sweet notes of Christmas carols. His heavy boots pounded across the creaking floorboards as he strode towards them.

"Ladies," his voice slithered like a lazy river. "How's it all going? The gym looks ... magnificent." He quickly scanned their work, his gaze shifting from one person to the other.

Chrissie forced a smile, trying to hide her irritation. "Thank you. Just putting the finishing touches on things."

He turned and greeted Denise with a smile. "Hello, Denise. Thank you for being a guardian of this town for so long, and I am eternally in your debt."

"Thank you. It doesn't take much…just doing my job," she answered.

In the colorful light, he grinned, displaying two rows of teeth that glistened. Stretching his arms out, he casually observed the room.

"You two have done a remarkable job here," he said, eyes boring into them with intensity. "I can't thank you enough for your dedication and commitment."

He abruptly strode away, his whistling carrying through the air.

After sharing a glance, the two erupted into loud laughter.

"You are the worst," Chrissie said, a smile lighting up her face.

"And you're a fucking pain in the ass," Denise retorted with a hearty laugh, shaking her head.

"So, tell me, will Haley come to this dance? Or will she remain too cool for us?"

Denise sighed. "I don't think so. She's been slaving away at that godforsaken Christmas Wonderland, trying to keep up the steady flow of money. I mean, she hates it. Gone are those days when her dad was here and money grew on trees. So much for teenage rebellion."

Chrissie snickered and gave Denise's shoulder a solid thump. "Yeah, I know; my teenager doesn't even look at his mama anymore; he thinks he's too cool now."

"That's his loss. Let's wrap this up and leave. I need to hit the sack soon. I have another twelve-hour shift tomorrow: day patrol and this silly dance. It's not like it'll be any fun either."

"No sweat. I'll take care of it. Don't forget the batch of cookies I made for you."

"Thanks, Chrissie. You never cease to amaze me. Sorry, I'm such a lazy bum when it comes to Christmas stuff."

Chrissie wrapped one arm around Denise in a hug. "You know how to make a girl feel special. But at the same time, you can be such a pain in the ass…"

Denise stepped back and crossed her arms over her chest. "Yep! Ain't no way I'm changing for nobody—not even my best friend!"

The women shared an amused glance as they made their way through the maze of chairs towards the exit.

Both of them were completely unaware of the events about to take place in their town.

Matt's Lie

MATT ALWAYS DREADED ENTERING his bedroom. Faded band posters were on the walls, and the stale food smelled. His X-box seemed to hum like an evil spirit - the relentless Call of Duty beckoning from its depths.

Lying to Haley about the dance left him feeling guilty and desperate. Not a single girl would talk to him. He saw her as the perfect woman. Independent, with her own apartment, and not living with her parents. His situation was the complete opposite of hers. He lived in his parents' house, bound to a room, and remained in his older brother's shadow.

As Matt peeled off the layers of his work attire, a gust of frigid air swirled through the room like a phantom. His brother Mike had crept up on him unawares, his eyes livid with loathing and contempt. Rasping through clenched teeth, he uttered an ultimatum.

"Fork over fifty bucks - now!"

Fury surged through Matt like a blazing inferno, sparks of hatred igniting his tongue.

"Hell no! Get yourself a goddamn job, you worthless piece of crap!"

Mike crossed the room in a heartbeat and pinned him on the bed. He growled into his ear with all the force of an avalanche, "Don't you ever dare talk to me like that again, you miserable little maggot! College isn't easy — I spent my last penny getting ready to take Tracey out for the dance tomorrow night. You should thank your stars you're still alive whenever I'm at home for the week!" His brother's foul breath hit Matt.

"FUCK YOU!"

Mike stood up abruptly and looked around the cramped room. The flashing Santa on the desk caught his attention.

"Christ," he said. "You still got this stupid fucking thing? You are an absolute moron. When are you going to grow up?"

"GET OUT!" Matt stood with fists clenched and brow knotted in wrathful indignation. "Get the fuck out of here, you loser!"

"Don't you tell me what to do, you little shit!"

Mike's smirk was sinister, and his every step echoed throughout the room, gaining momentum. His face contorted into a grotesque mask of hate as he leaned closer to his brother, and his fists shook uncontrollably with rage. Even though Matt knew that resistance would only make matters worse, he desperately steeled himself for a fight, bracing himself for the onslaught of Mike's wrath.

Matt's voice was a desperate plea, his disbelief palpable as he tried to reason with Mike one last time.

"What's wrong, anyway? You come home for Christmas break, and suddenly, you're an entirely different person." His words hung in the air, full of confusion and frustration.

"You don't know what it's like, Matt. All this pressure and stress from school? It's relentless. Do you think I chose this life? It is Dad's dream, not mine. Don't kid yourself."

"Well, I guess I can loan you some money, but pay me back before you go back to school, dude," Matt said reluctantly.

"Yeah, thanks, bro. Now finish up, nerd, and come downstairs. Mom and Dad have some Christmas crap they want to do. Mom just put out a batch of her homemade cookies." He gave Matt a rough shove before turning and striding out.

Scanning the room made Matt's stomach churn. It was proof that Mike was right about him being a nerd. In one corner, Star Wars action figures glowered from their unopened packages, as if ready to ambush anyone stupid enough to enter. On top of his dresser, rows of Pokemon figurines lined up, stiff and uniform, like some miniature army waiting for orders to march into battle. Despite his age, Matt appeared stuck in a bygone era where toys were everything and adulthood was a distant dream.

To Matt, Mike was an unstoppable force of nature. His presence charmed females, his athletic achievements were a tribute to his glory. In contrast, Matt felt trapped in his parents' Elview house, with no chance of college because of his terrible grades, and no promising job prospects.

The intense insanity that his mother exhibited, and her all-consuming obsession with the upcoming Christmas dance, had Matt reeling in shock. He firmly believed that her life relied on being the head of the decorating committee. Her enthusiasm for mundane holiday festivities seemed to have no end, and it horrified him.

His phone buzzed, jolting him from his thoughts, and he clumsily retrieved it. His heart quickened as it unlocked, and the words filling the screen caused him a frenzied anticipation. Haley's message stirred something profound inside — a warmth that spread through his chest, causing a smile to crest his lips.

Guess I'll go for a little while ... don't want to get on Santa's bad list lol

A strange feeling of dread ran through him as he set to work on the reply. He tried to come up with something witty or clever, but all that came out were some feeble words that felt inadequate to him.

Awesome, see you there. Work sure sucked, didn't it?

He watched as the illuminated dots bounced across the screen, showing an incoming text.

Yup. You still going there with your hot date?

His finger hovered over the send button as despair and dread warred in his heart. He knew if he pressed it, he'd be lying to her. She'd think he was still single and a loser if he didn't. But what choice did he have? Taking a deep breath of resignation, he clicked 'send' with an empty, *You know it.*

Well, I will be there. You better make time for your work bestie, and I am excited to meet her.

He swallowed hard as he typed back a response, forcing himself to sound content.

Sure thing, was all he could muster.

Now, the guilt weighed heavily on his conscience; what had seemed like a good idea at the time was an albatross around his neck. He hurriedly dressed and made his way down the stairs with trepidation. His mother was in the kitchen, the inviting smell of freshly baked cookies filling the air, but it did little to quell his nerves.

The Dance

Christmas Eve

As she drove through the downtown area, Denise felt despair. Every inhalation of air felt like knives piercing her broken heart from losing her husband and dashing any hopes of a happy Christmas now that Haley had left home to start her own life in town. Now, she isolated herself on this defiled holy evening.

But there was an unspoken solace in her work. The annual Christmas Dance for the community would take place tonight, and Denise thought of her friend Chrissie, who had always been overly exuberant about the festivities.

Then memories came flooding back from decades ago when Denise had been reckless and wild, never dreaming that destiny would lead her to become a cop. A sly smirk crept across her face.

She eased her cruiser into the Christmas Wonderland parking lot, her headlights shining over the glittering snow. Reaching for the frosted cookies that Chrissie had given her, she stuffed them hungrily into her mouth as she gulped down bitter coffee from a paper cup. Though the two had been through thick and thin, things between them seemed to have changed lately. Her gaze peered down to see Chrissie's name across the screen of her phone. She set aside the tins of freshly baked cookies and swiped her finger against the screen.

Hey girl, Chrissie's message read, *I hope you will make it tonight, at least for a while. What could happen in this dingy little town of ours?*

Of course, I should make it over for a little while, Denise typed back with a smiley face, then added, *Those cookies were amazing!*

A few seconds later came a reply.

Can't wait to see you here! It's quite a party.

She grinned and typed, *Give me about thirty minutes, and I'll make my grand entrance.*

You got it, old timer! See you soon.

She turned the key, and the cruiser's engine roared. Elview's Christmas decorations cast a warm yellow glow over the snow-covered cobblestone pathways.

She squinted through the swirling vortex of snow, her eyes settling on Ben Chase — the town drunk. He staggered down the street, his hoodie a flimsy shield against the frigid weather. She slowed the car and rolled down the window.

"Hey, Ben," she shouted over the wind's howling wail.

With a grunt, he lumbered over to her open window and leaned in; the smell of whiskey seeping from his every pore made her recoil. "Hello, officer."

"Do you need a ride? It is freezing out here."

Ben was silent for what felt like an eternity, eying her curiously. "Uhhh," he finally mumbled, "Nah, I'm cool. Gonna' walk if you don't mind."

"Ben, it's awful out here! Please let me give you a ride. I'm not trying to start any trouble. I want to make sure that you're safe."

He remained standing, his face stiff and unmoving, as he watched her with a wary eye. "No, this is nothing. It's nothing compared to what I've seen before."

She gazed at him with understanding, empathizing with his life of hardship.

"Fine, suit yourself," she said. "Have a good Christmas."

He said nothing, only giving her an icy nod before turning away. She stomped on the gas pedal and drove off, feeling her tires slip against the icy road.

The car had a discordant harmony of holiday music and windshield wipers. A voice suddenly spoke over the dispatch like an electric shock.

She did not know that the message she would receive would unleash far darker and more sinister forces than anything her mind could have ever dreamed of.

Haley emerged from her car, struggling against the insidious winter chill. Her red sweater was like a flimsy shield against the oncoming darkness and howling wind. Her blue hair shimmered like sapphires. She approached the building cautiously, the snow crunching beneath her feet. It appeared to be sentient and watching her, almost alive and aware of her wrongdoings. A wave of heat greeted her as she opened the door.

An icy fear tightened its grip around Haley's heart as she realized the true meaning of Elview's holiday celebration. With forced smiles, they all pretended nothing was wrong, but everyone knew the truth: a dark and inescapable terror had descended upon Elview on Christmas Eve decades before. Though rumors swirled, nobody dared to whisper what killed those innocent people; some spoke of extraterrestrial forces, while others suspected government experiments. No one would ever uncover the truth.

Haley's heart thudded in her chest as she entered, passionate teenagers' eyes fixed on her. Her face grew hot. She felt as if all the hallways scrutinized her, an icy energy radiating from their stares. Taking a deep breath to steady her shaking body, Haley hastened towards the gym entrance, her footsteps echoing like thunder through the linoleum floor. A foul amalgam of sweat and fresh paint polluted the air, sticking into her throat like tar. Cheerful decorations hung from the walls, and festive sounds blared from within the gym, but nothing could ease the tension that had settled around Haley.

She stared in repulsion as the couples moved around the dance floor, the men like vultures and the women helplessly clinging to them. The band onstage, dressed like elves, plowed through off-key holiday songs with an almost malicious glee. Everything about it was a nightmare come true.

She surveyed the area, and her eyes settled on a tall, strapping figure. He had a possessive hold on an attractive woman, his expression stern. His clean white collared shirt hugged his muscular physique and showcased the fullness of his shoulders.

"Hey there, Haley," he purred in a velvety tone, "Do you remember me?" With a flourish, he disengaged from the other girl and extended his hand for a handshake.

"Hi Mike," she spat defensively while his date steamed away in a huff.

"I have never figured out what you see in my brother," he said, edging closer and closer until she could absorb all of him — perceiving how strikingly he resembled Matt in looks, but sturdier and taller.

"Where is that brother of yours? He's the one who makes me feel like an absolute loser if I choose not to show up at this idiotic event."

"He's around here somewhere."

Haley's eyes darted to the gym entrance, where Matt stood looking forlorn in a drab brown sports coat and an old Santa hat. A pang of empathy stirred within her as Mike led her over and smacked his brother hard on the shoulder.

"Hey, dufus, your friend Haley is here. How about you not be a loser and say hello," he said, before turning away to join his pneumatic date standing near the dance floor.

Haley shot Mike an icy glare, then turned to Matt with a smile.

"Hey, Matt, Merry Christmas and all that shit."

Matt fidgeted with his phone while looking at her averted face. He mumbled lamely, "Hi, Haley. Sorry if my brother was rude; I swear he's not always like that."

They moved closer to the punch bowl, the crappy Christmas music blaring in their ears.

"So, what happened to your date, Matt? And do you know where I could find one of my own?"

Matt shook his head, looking down at his feet.

"Sorry, I asked her a week ago, and she just ... I dunno never called back or replied to my texts or something." He shuddered, eyes locked on her gaze.

"Let's have some fun, then. Who needs a date when I can just get savagely drunk and forget my troubles?" she snickered, her voice sweet as honey.

His head jolted upwards in surprise at her words, and she shyly glanced away. The oppressive silence that followed was palpable until she reached out and gripped his hand with a sudden urgency.

"Look, I'm starving, but we're already here," she laughed maniacally. "Might as well mingle."

The lead singer's banshee-like wail soared above the instruments' din as the band started their rendition of 'Christmas In Hollis.' A portly man wearing a Santa costume and a bedazzled vest spoke unintelligibly while the audience watched.

"My God! It sounds like the band never even bothered to rehearse," Haley told Matt over the clamor of clashing chords.

Matt scoffed and rolled his eyes.

"What do you expect? This is Elview, after all."

Her fingers dug into his arm like talons. She nodded her head at something beyond the buffet table.

"See that?"

He followed her gaze and saw two figures: a young woman with hair of flame standing beside an older woman dressed in denim and Doc Martens.

"Emily Carroll and her grandmother," Haley whispered. "Local legends. They stir up trouble with loony online conspiracy theorists every Christmas."

Matt's eyes widened in disbelief.

"Holy shit, yeah, the grandmother lived through whatever happened here in the eighties."

"Yes!" The throbbing of instruments drowned out Haley's ragged voice. "She visited one of my classes last semester and told us about aliens! A complete crackpot ..."

A shudder ran through Matt as he turned and saw an apparition trundling towards them. She wore a candy cane-striped outfit that covered her body in a patchwork fashion, struggling to contain the roundness of her bosom. As she walked, Matt moaned deeply.

"Oh no, it's my mom," he whimpered.

Haley extended her hand.

"Happy Holidays, Mrs. Bowen."

The woman cast her gaze on Haley like a blade of cold steel. Matt shifted his feet in discomfort and averted his eyes.

"Ahh, Haley, I see you finally showed up," chirped Mrs. Bowen with the voice of a viper. "Forget about all that Mrs. Bowen nonsense. You have known me forever. Just call me Chrissie."

"Okay," Haley replied.

"Your mother sent me a text that she'd be back from her patrol soon, so don't even think about misbehaving," she cackled, her crooked eyes burrowing deep into Haley's soul.

Haley bit down on her lip to stifle a laugh. "My mom, a hard-nosed guardian of the peace. What would we do without her?"

"No doubt about that," Chrissie cackled. "But she can be a good friend, too."

Matt suddenly cut in, attempting to change the subject, "We were just hanging out and talking, Mom."

As Matt spoke, he nervously adjusted the collar of his shirt, and Chrissie surveyed him with her usual disdain. Her eyes lingered on his attire and the unkempt hair that framed his face.

Haley watched and wished she could evaporate into thin air.

Chrissie leaned into Haley, her breath a cocktail of peppermint and whiskey. Haley fought to keep from retching. "Listen here. I'm sure you know I can be intense, but all I want is the best for my son. He's not a kid anymore, and he likes you."

A surge of fury and embarrassment shot through Haley's veins. Before she could respond, Matt spoke up.

"What are you whispering about?"

Chrissie's head snapped up, and she glowered at her son, her voice as sharp as a shard of glass. "Nothing, dear. Are you having fun?" She turned to Haley with a saccharine smile and said, "Excuse us; I'm going to get him out there dancing!"

Matt shook his head in defiance. His mother refused to accept his refusal and clamped an iron grip around his wrist, dragging him towards the dance floor like a rag doll in the hands of an unstoppable force. He shuffled along reluctantly, his face twisted into a mask of terror.

Haley was stunned that such an appalling woman could be responsible for something as beautiful as her son. She followed his every move, her heart clenching, until he finally disappeared into the mad cacophony of lights, festive holiday tunes, and chaotic commotion.

Gloria's Past

GLORIA LURKED IN THE dim shadows of the dance floor. Emily's twirls and laughter held her attention. Though Gloria was struggling internally, the sight of her granddaughter, a stunning young woman with unlimited potential, made her smile. She secretly poured a generous portion of vodka from a flask in her purse into her punch glass. She lifted it in a silent salute to the ceiling.

"Here's to you, Sam. A perfect friend," she rasped.

Fear had clung to Gloria like a pall since the incident on Christmas Eve of 1986. Her anxiety and protectiveness of those she loved colored every day. First Marcus, now Emily. Each time the latter ventured out, Gloria held her breath as if it was the last time she would ever see her again.

YULETIDE INVASION

Gloria had been in government hands for almost a year, after the out-of-this-world visitors descended on Elview. She remembered her best friend Sam's selfless sacrifice to keep them all safe from the aliens, and their escape. She felt the cage of fear tightening around her each day, worried that someone would discover the mysterious extraterrestrial code inside herself — a secret she'd kept even from her deceased husband.

Emily's shoes skidded across the creaky hardwood as she rushed in, panting and flushed with excitement. Two other girls followed like shadows behind her, their eyes wide with anticipation.

"I wanted you to meet my new friends, Rachel and Lily!" Emily exclaimed, her voice high-pitched with joy.

"It's so nice to meet you both," she said, extending a hand for each girl to shake.

Emily beamed from ear to ear. "My Grandma is the coolest! She's like a real badass!"

"I don't know about that. I do my best to keep up with you young folks." She reached out and briefly ruffled Emily's hair with a tender touch.

Then Gloria felt an arctic shiver ripple, like someone had just walked over to her grave. Goosebumps shot up her arms, and she cast a wary eye around the room. She didn't know what exactly she was searching for, but something seemed to stir within the shadows of the partygoers, and she couldn't shake the feeling that something awful lurked in their midst.

Emily noticed her grandmother's quivering hands, illuminated by the red-green pulsations of the holiday lights. The band played 'Jingle Bell Rock' with a nearly insane intensity.

Emily's hand hovered over her grandmother's arm, barely touching it. She spoke in a low whisper, "Are you alright?".

"Yes, yes," Gloria responded almost robotically, trying to force a small smile as she lied.

"A-are you thinking of the story you tell y-you every Ch-Christmas? The one where your friend Sam ... died?"

Gloria's face contorted into sheer terror, and Emily immediately knew something was amiss. Her grandmother had never been keen on lies — but these words were more than they seemed. A darkness in Gloria's eyes told Emily there was something else lurking beneath the surface.

"I'm a little jumpy," Gloria said. Without a second thought, Emily gently grasped her grandmother's arm.

"It's alright. I know it's still hard for you around Christmas time." Her face wrinkled with concern. "But you can always talk to me if you need anything, okay?"

Gloria nodded, unable to find the words to express how relieved she felt at her granddaughter's unwavering support. "Okay then," she said, "we'll stick together."

Gloria shuddered as her gaze traveled throughout the gym. She felt something was amiss in this place, and whatever it was would be far more sinister than any fear she had ever endured.

Carla awoke with a howl, her flesh burning like a thousand needles shoved into her. The air was thick with an otherworldly fog, and a chill cut through her bones. Her disoriented eyes finally adjusted to the sight of her naked body exposed to the world in a car, and she shivered as an eerie azure hue lit up the night.

Numbly, she felt a sensation in her midsection - something wet, warm, and sticky. Something had crudely sewn together a wound on her stomach with thick thread, and it was oozing hot, foul-smelling blood.

And then came the creeping sensation of something coiling around her mind, pushing away all her logic and reason. It seemed as if she had been asleep for eons, trapped in a waking nightmare.

Snow had transformed the car into a cocoon of frost. Carla got her first glimpse of it, and she gasped with fear. Her fingers trembled as she donned her clothing hastily, including her thick winter coat. But none of these could keep out the icy chill that crawled through her bones or stop the sensation of being watched by an unseen force within the darkness.

Searing agony ripped through her skull as the abomination inside of her stirred. Its squirming body slithered from her gut to fill her veins, then shot into her mind, no longer content to lurk in secrecy. It desired complete domination.

She pushed open the car door with such force that it almost ripped from its hinges. A burst of fierce arctic air hit her in the face. Her body fought to stay upright while her feet slid on the snowy pavement.

She gasped in a deep breath, the cold air tearing into her lungs like fire. The snow, which reached her thighs with every step she took, devoured her feet. Searching desperately for anything to clutch onto, all she felt were her frozen hands crunched cruelly against the empty air. Darkness swirled around her, threatening to sweep her away at any moment.

The bone-chilling force of vile tendrils constricted her muscles, slithering up her spine from an unfathomable thing. Her arms were as heavy as leaden boulders, hanging by her sides, anchored by an unseen force. An insatiable hunger consumed her from within, relentlessly gnawing at her belly. She took a few steps forward, moving like a marionette.

With each step through the snow, Carla's will weakened. It smothered her mind in a dense fog, numbing her senses and slowing her actions. Her vision blurred, and she felt herself on the edge of sanity.

Abruptly, the sight of Frank startled her. He lay dormant against a stark white canvas, his eyes empty and lifeless, his mouth open in a silent scream, with frozen blood dripping from his lips. Entrails of death and carnage encircled his body like an unholy halo. He was now a grotesque ice sculpture shifting against a graveyard of snow.

A gut-wrenching scream clawed up her throat, determined to force its way out. But something within her wouldn't let it escape. It kept her mute and immobile, as a creature of unknown origin possessed her body, denying her the opportunity for one last tender caress of Frank's face.

The power of the unknown entity bound, paralyzed, and chained her to its every demand. She felt her will slip away like water through a sieve as it tightened its grasp on her mind, overwhelming her with a force she could not fight against. Bit by bit, her autonomy faded until nothing remained but an empty shell, enslaved by this invisible terror.

The hunger inside Carla's skull was insatiable, driving her forward to satisfy its need. It sought bodies — many of them — to fill with its spawn. The thing dug into Carla's mind and found what it sought — a horde of unsuspecting victims ripe for the taking. Her steps quickened as she moved closer to her prey.

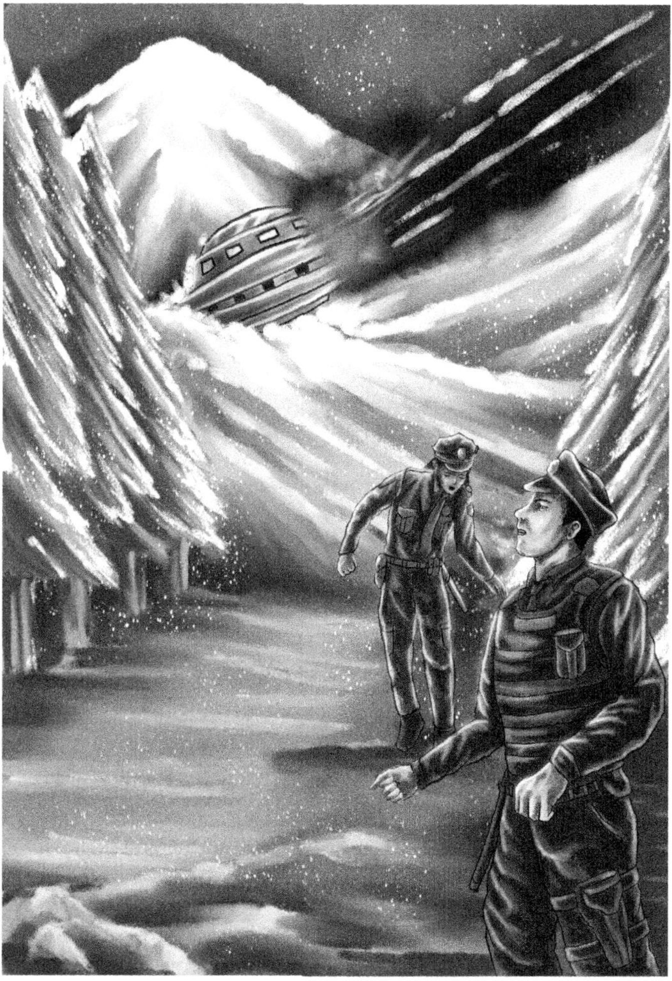

The Thing In Carla

A DECREPIT BUICK CHUGGED its way through the snowdrifts like an ancient beast, belching exhaust and rocking on worn shocks. It closed in on Carla, a 'My Kid Is An Honor Student' sticker plastered to its dented bumper. Slamming on its brakes with a squeal, the vehicle shuddered to a stop beside her. The driver's window lowered, and a large man with patchy facial hair and wild red curls peered out. His eyes gleamed from his ratty flannel coat as he looked at Carla. His voice was like serrated blades slicing through the air, and his lips curved in a smirk. "Whatcha doin' out here, sweetheart? No one should be alone on Christmas Eve. Hop in my car — let's get you someplace warm and spread some holiday cheer."

Carla locked eyes with him, her gaze almost feral. She could feel something foreign inside of her, desperate for release. The words came out slowly and detached as she spoke.

"Yes. I would like that." For a moment, all was still. Then, an unnatural calm washed over her. In a monotonous tone, she added, "Thank you."

The rusty door groaned as the man opened it for Carla. She clambered in without a word, daring him with her eyes not to ask. But he spoke anyway, his gravelly voice like a blade.

"What in tarnation are you doin' out here this time of night? Not a safe place for young girls like yerself."

Carla replied calmly, "My car broke down, and I was heading to the Christmas dance."

"I've never been to one of those. Hated school and Christmas ain't my thing." The man sneered, his beady eyes surveying her.

The creature inhabiting Carla's body searched for a response once more. "It's ... a lot of fun."

He cleared his throat. "Where are you comin' from?"

"I... I don't remember."

"You sure are a looker," he said, quickly flicking his eyes from the road to her and back.

Carla could feel his gaze crawling over her skin like a thousand ants, aware of a growing bulge in his pants.

"No man at all?" he continued, clearly pleased with himself.

She was silent momentarily before replying quietly, "Not anymore."

The car halted, and Carla jolted forward in her seat. The stranger's eyes glinted in the low light of the dashboard as he turned to face her, his hand creeping up her thigh with an animalistic hunger.

"Looks like you won't be making it to that Christmas dance," he chuckled, voice thick with desire. "But don't worry, I'll make sure you have a good time."

An otherworldly fire surged within her. It was an inferno that eloped from the depths of her being, speaking through her voice like a divine force. "Okay, baby."

The man lunged at her with rabid ferocity, tearing away her clothing as he ravished her delicate curves with his hands and lips. There was nothing tender about his movements -—only an insatiable and overwhelming hunger that demanded satisfaction. He pinned her onto the car seat, pressing against every inch of her petite frame, while Carla grabbed his face and crushed her mouth into his.

In an instant, he recoiled, horrified by the sensation of something slithering inside him — thousands of tiny snakes wriggling in his chest and squeezing in his throat. Hair-like feelers violated his flesh, flooding him with a swarm of frenzied larvae before Carla's hand shot down his pants, clamping around his cock in a savage grip that tore it free from its fleshy prison with one final jerk. He spasmed as blood sprayed across the car seat.

Her tentacles shot forward, coiling around him like snakes. A large writhing tendril surrounded him and lifted him off the seat. With a forceful thrust, she snapped his neck.

Yanking the driver's door with a powerful motion, she heaved the body from the seat, sending it crashing onto the snow-covered street below. She then turned the key in the ignition. The engine roared to life like some feral beast awakened from its slumber.

The narrow, winding road was lit by the white beams of the headlights, shining like searchlights in the dark. Elvis Presley's 'Blue Christmas' played like an ominous omen. She sensed the entity within her, eager for new flesh to consume, and she knew what would sate it.

<hr>

Denise's teeth chattered as the frigid air kissed her skin. Her partner Peter pushed onward, his boots trudging through the deep snow, leaving a trail of footprints. He sealed his lips shut, making no sound except for the crunching of his steps in the hardened drifts.

"What the fuck is this about, Peter?" she asked, her eyes flashing between him and the unrelenting snowstorm that filled their vision. Her face was now laced with icy snowflakes, and she checked the time with a frustrated grunt.

"Damnit, Denise," Peter cursed as the north wind howled around them. "I should be at home eatin' a big ol' ham my wife cooked up for Christmas Eve. Instead, I'm wanderin' in this winter wasteland on the verge of starvin' to death."

Peter shivered as he spoke, still trudging forward.

"Been a good ten minutes since the call came through. They saw some shady business goin' on, and sure enough, we got us a murder. Now, this is where things get nuts, cos it turns out to be Frank Bundick's corpse lyin' there in a pool of blood. And lemme tell you somethin'. What I saw would make the hardest soul quiver with fear. Now, believe me, I've seen my share of gruesome scenes, but this one? It takes the cake."

As the only law enforcement personnel in Elview, Denise and Peter rarely encountered violent incidents. Fate dealt them a terrible hand tonight. It was like a sucker punch, and it surprised Denise. For months, she had planned to attend the dance and spend time with her daughter Haley. This vicious crime in the dark shattered the moment.

"Holy Hell!" she hissed, her eyes widening as they beheld the lifeless form before them.

Peter nodded slowly, his face deathly pale.

Her stomach churned as she examined Frank's corpse, twisted and mangled. Her voice was a low whisper. "That is one sick son of a bitch. What kind of monster could do something like this?" Her flashlight reflected off the car, its door hanging from its hinge like a broken bone, intensifying her dread. "What in God's name happened here?"

Denise's flashlight beam shined across the darkness, finally resting on a vast abyss. It seemed to stretch out endlessly, punctuated here and there with jagged bits of metal reflecting the light. Her arm shook rigidly as she pointed into the impenetrable blackness, her finger quivering wildly in fear of what might lurk within. The sight was beyond strange.

"What is that?" Peter asked, squinting into the darkness.

Denise crept forward, her figure a pale specter in the snow. Peter followed, unable to look away from her ghostly form. His boots sank into the snow as he nervously ventured onward. Ahead of them was a barely visible ridge of dirt and snow encircling an immense, glowing, saucer-shaped object. The fear gripped his chest as he moved closer, feeling so minuscule compared to its grandness. He was aware of what it heralded and prayed he was wrong.

"I ... do not know," she said, her fingers flexing about her gun in its holster.

He took a step forward. His boots crackled with each crunching step, as if snapping at him to turn back. A frigid breeze encircled them like a spectral vanguard. His eyes bulged as he gazed upon the destruction before him.

"Maybe it was a goddamn meteor?"

The pair crept closer to the crater, spilling smoke and steam like a devil's cauldron. Embers flared and melted the surrounding snow.

"This sure as hell is no meteor, Peter."

Peter ventured into the unknown, his bravado barely masking his fear. He thrust away the billowing smoke as if it were a living thing.

"It looks like ..." He backed away slowly. "It looks like a God-damned flying saucer! Jesus!"

Denise stared at him in disbelief, her fists clenched tightly. "Not this horseshit again!"

Peter was trembling. "What do we do?"

Denise flinched, her countenance curdling into a grimace. "We have to report this, Pete. We can't let them come back here like they did last time." She hugged herself against the mounting chill as the snow swirled around them. "Lock this place down and ask no questions," she went on through gritted teeth, her hand hovering dangerously close to the Glock strapped to her thigh.

"Something ain't right here, that's for damn sure."

"Call the goddamn Wyoming County Sheriff's Office! Now!" she ordered. "I need to get to that dance. If something bad happens at such a big event in this town, it'll be on my head. That poor old fucker, Mitch Logan, is our only chance of stopping whatever shit is about to go down, but he looks like an ancient corpse already."

"You got it." His voice reverberated through the night air, a warning that seemed to carry an unspoken doom. "Be careful!"

"You too," she shouted back fiercely, just before being swallowed up by the all-encompassing shadows and billowing snowflakes disappearing into a flurry of snow and ice.

Peter slowly spun around to take in the destruction before him, struggling to comprehend what had happened. His mind swarmed with questions, yet one thought was deafening - why did this occur on Christmas Eve?

The Hatching

The car spat snow from beneath its tires as it crawled through the snow-filled parking lot. The headlights pierced the darkness only to illuminate a bleak landscape of white silhouettes and undulating drifts. But Carla felt something emanating from a building up ahead — an aura of anticipation that brought an electric shiver down her spine. Even alone, she could sense those who witnessed her ascension — the Progenitress of a new breed.

The thumping beat of music echoed like a heartbeat from the building walls as she parked and got out. She felt a writhing sensation that filled her with anticipation. Trembling, she eagerly anticipated unveiling what she had nurtured and safeguarded within herself.

By the entrance, a lit-up Santa loomed faceless with a sickly glow of red and green. The roof and windows had strings of multicolored bulbs that hung like nooses, casting an eerie light into the darkness. Flickering letters on a sign invited all to the Christmas Dance. Down the path, two figures embraced while four others shared an e-cigarette, its vapor swirling through the freezing air.

An intimidating presence filled the doorway to the school. The man was a titan, tall and dark-skinned, with eyes that showed his many years. He had candy canes on his vest and a snow-white coronet on his bald head.

"Greetings, young lady." His voice oozed with kindness. "Let me see that wristband of yours."

The creature inside Carla frantically scrambled to find a response. "I... I lost it," she stammered. "I went outside for some air."

He grinned widely, his eyes twinkling with joy as he nodded in affirmation.

"No worries. I hope you're enjoying the holidays. Merry Christmas!" His voice softened as he offered her his hand. "Mitch."

She felt a tingling sensation course through her body and curled into his touch, offering him a grateful smile.

"Thank you, Mitch. And Merry Christmas to you as well," Carla said before turning towards the gymnasium, where she could hear the voices of dozens of revelers inside dancing along with the beat of a discordant melody.

The fire burning inside her had become undeniable, a hunger that consumed her soul and scratched at her sanity. The fire burning inside her left nothing but an incandescent rage, and what remained of the old Carla was a hollow shell. They were now out there, hiding in the shadows of the snowdrifts. It would soon unleash them, a horde of creatures freed from her consuming darkness.

And they would gorge on flesh...

Haley watched as the wraith-like figure of Carla glided into the party alone. The gossip whispered that she and Frank Bundick were still an item — amazingly resilient, given her lurid past with the entire football team, or so it seemed. Carla's complexion was pallid in the dimly lit hall, and her greasy locks stuck to her skin.

Most notable were her eyes — a sickeningly bright shade of red-rimmed pink. Haley had never seen her this disheveled. Carla stopped directly before her and offered a wide grin, but there was something peculiar about her expression, as if she was seeking someone or something.

"Hello Haley, long time no see. How are you? I mean, how is life for you?"

She hovered too close, the stench of body odor and something dark rolling off her in a thick cloud. It smelled like Carla had been bathing in blood, and like a giant shit that had festered in a toilet bowl for too long. Haley noticed brown and red streaks on her face and hands like slashes of paint amidst a dying backdrop of white skin gone sickly gray in the dim light.

"I am living the dream, ya know, just trying to get through the holiday season," Haley replied, stepping back from Carla's overpowering presence. "But are you okay? I don't mean to sound rude, but you don't look so good."

A couple dancing bumped into Carla as they passed by. She didn't budge, her body stiff and unresponsive to the impact. Her expression was blank, eyes glassy and vacant.

"Thank you for asking," Carla said in an emotionless tone. "I just have been feeling a little under the weather, but I didn't want to miss this. You know that the whole town seems to stop everything for this stupid thing, ya know?"

Haley looked at Carla, whose eyes seemed to dart around the room in fear. Something is really off with Carla, she thought to herself.

The lights flickered and then dimmed, followed by an ear-piercing buzz and feedback screeching through the speakers. Everyone stopped dancing, and heads turned to search for the noise source.

"Sorry about that, folks. Not sure what happened there. I guess it was technical difficulties. Maybe Santa's elves!" the singer quipped, trying to lighten the mood.

But the atmosphere in the room had drastically changed. It was as if a chill had descended over them all. The music started again, but it seemed like an eerie soundtrack to the dread lingering in the air. Haley felt her skin prickle with anxiety as she watched Carla move off into the crowd, her movements almost robotic and strange.

Matt walked up to her, his strides long and easy. He ran a hand through his hair, disheveling it slightly as he leaned in close.

"Hey you," he said, his voice low, "I finally ditched my mom. Jesus, I am an adult now, and she still clings to me like I am a toddler. I need to get the fuck out of my parents' house." He glanced around before continuing, "You look pretty amazing tonight, by the way. Have you danced yet?" He held out his hand, palm up in invitation.

Haley swallowed hard, her eyes scanning the room for Carla. She took Matt's hand and followed him to the dance floor.

The melody of the Christmas song plodded along sentimentally, but Haley couldn't process the music or dancing. Carla's icy glare burned into her back like a branding iron, making her stiffen in Matt's embrace. He leaned closer and brushed his lips against her earlobe.

"Can you enjoy yourself now?" he whispered, breath hot on her skin.

"It's getting better," she replied.

He smiled at her as they moved to the beat. "Might be cheesy for me to say this," he said, eyes twinkling, "But I like all this Christmas stuff."

"You're always ready with those corny lines, huh? But yeah, it still sucks."

"Come on, Haley, let go of your inhibitions. It's Christmas Eve. Let's have some fun."

Haley trembled, feeling a heat rise from inside her core. She felt something awaken within her — something wild and untamed. Even though she had fantasized about Matt for years, they had never been beyond friendship ... until now. The moody atmosphere of the room seemed to beckon her forward, to reach out and seize the moment.

Their lips met, and a shudder ran through her. His hands felt like fire on either side of her face, his fingers curling around her hair as he pulled the kiss deeper. The mistletoe hung above them like a macabre symbol of fate. They broke apart, Haley offering a devilish smirk.

"How's that for fun?" she chuckled darkly.

"That's more like it."

"You know I've always really had the hots for you," she said with a husky whisper, looking up into his eyes. "My favorite cursed soul in this wretched town."

His face reddened as he averted his eyes. "I guess there's not much competition."

She grinned. "Maybe it's the holidays or this stupid mistletoe above us."

He flashed her a crooked smile that faded quickly.

"Been sweet on you since high school, Haley," he said. "Just didn't want you thinkin' I'm some desperado — so yeah, about that date tonight? That was all made up."

"Oh, Matt," she said, her eyes twinkling with delight. She pulled his hands into hers and squeezed them. "You are a big old dork, aren't ya?"

He grabbed her by the shoulders, pressing her close as he said, "Merry Christmas, Haley," and then planted another kiss on her lips.

But as their lips touched, the warmth of Matt's kiss suddenly drained away, and Haley felt a strange unease. She looked over his shoulder and saw Carla standing across the room. Her body convulsed in chaotic spasms that contorted her limbs out of shape, while drool cascaded from her mouth like a leaking faucet. Her eyes were wide and unmoving, fixed on a distant point above Haley's head.

"What the hell?" Matt said, following Haley's gaze to Carla alone on the other side of the room. "What's wrong with her?"

A thud echoed throughout the crowd as Carla stumbled and crashed against the hardwood floor.

Haley's terror rose like a wave, crashing over her as she and Matt fought through the bodies on the dance floor. Finally reaching Carla, they found her writhing in frenzied, horrific convulsions, her bulging eyes transfixed with horror and thick crimson foam spilling from her gaping mouth. It was as if she had peered into the abyss, and it had consumed her whole.

The audience grew quiet, as though under a spell. The band stopped playing abruptly. All eyes locked on Carla.

A woman with a garishly oversized holiday sweater, her features unmistakably Asian, was frantically waving her arms and giving an urgent plea to the horde of people gathering around her.

"Call 911!" Her voice came out unsteadily as she shouted. "Everyone! Get back!"

The woman dropped to her knees, determined to do whatever it took to save Carla's life. Carla's body continued writhing as more seizures wracked her limbs, and dark shapes bulged from beneath her skin.

A fleshy tentacle erupted from Carla's chest with unholy force. It thrashed in a grotesque dance, spraying the room with vile fluids. Before anyone could process what was happening, an abomination crawled out of her abdomen, bones cracking like thunder as it unraveled and skittered away.

The woman bending over Carla emitted a blood-curdling screech as wriggling tentacles slithered around her petite frame, like anacondas poised to devour their prey. In a sickening display, her head suddenly shot off from her neck with a loud pop like a cork released from a champagne bottle, splattering the watching crowd with a fountain of blood that seemed to fall through the air in agonizing slow motion.

Haley and Matt clung to each other; their fingers intertwined in terror. The room went pitch black, creating an atmosphere of dread. With every passing second, the quiet whimpers and sobs became louder, almost painfully echoing in Haley's ears as her heart hammered against her ribs like a madman beating on his cell walls.

A deep, menacing rumble filled the air, shaking the walls of the dark room. Haley's pulse quickened as the sound of metal scraping against stone crept in and grew louder. She felt an oppressive force edging closer. She cautiously called out.

"Matt?" Her voice quivered, her heart pounding harder in her chest. The darkness was overwhelming, and she clawed at the air, blindly searching for him. "We need to get out of here now," she said desperately.

"I can't see!" he replied.

As her eyes adjusted, the tentacles shot out from the center of the room, long and black like oil-soaked whips. They twisted and spun in every direction, slicing through the air with a whistling sound. Haley and Matt ducked beneath tables, dodging the oncoming appendages as screams filled the room. The crowd stampeded for exits, knocking over chairs and tables to escape.

"Haley!!!" Matt shrieked as they scrambled over the heaving, shuddering mass of people. "We gotta get outta here!"

Over the moans and shrieks, Haley heard a deep, unfamiliar voice chanting an indecipherable language.

Matt grabbed her arm. "Come on! We have to get out of here before we die!"

They clawed at the writhing tentacles, battering them with raw fists as they tried to escape. Another blood-curdling scream pierced the hall, sending a chill of fear up Haley's spine. An ominous presence lurched closer, its heat shivering over her skin and the putrid stench of death wafting through the air. People surged past her in vain panic, their screams becoming mute under the cacophony of snapping bones and wet splatters. There was an almighty thud, and a pleading female voice cried out, "No! Please!".

"This way!" Haley shouted, dragging Matt toward a shadow-cloaked hallway. Her eyes gleamed with determination as she led him closer to their destination, an old janitor's closet that held fond memories from her youth.

Despite the dim light, they noticed Mitch struggling through the crowd. His left arm clamped tightly to his chest, and a scarlet liquid cascaded from his hands.

"Run!" he screamed frantically. "They'll kill us all!"

As Mitch stumbled, a massive lithic creature loomed beside him. Its body was tall and sinewy, with an ashen gray-blue leathery hide. Two black eyes glinted like a somber hunter in the darkness. Long, tentacle-like protrusions jutted from its head.

A tentacle lashed out from the beast's maw and drove into Mitch's neck, slavering him to the ground in a shower of blood and viscera. The horror born from Carla's broken corpse scuttled across the room at unnatural speed and draped itself upon Mitch's face, feasting eagerly on his flesh.

The dance floor erupted into a further cacophony of screams and terror as an unearthly horde burst through the open doorway. The hideous aliens mindlessly beat and bludgeoned the petrified partygoers, crushing skulls and gorging on their brains like some monstrous feast. A stomach-churning blend of viscera and carnage followed in their wake as they drooled and lapped up rivers of crimson blood.

Matt gaped in dread as the ravenous throng of alien arachnids enveloped his brother and girlfriend, tearing at them.

"Oh, Jesus!" he gasped as Haley yanked him away from the slaughter.

"Come on!" she screamed, barely audible over the abominations' onslaught.

Everywhere they ran, tentacles destroyed everything in their path, slashing through even metal structures like ribbons.

The broken flesh rearranged, forming unrecognizable abominations as the dead stirred and writhed. Bones twisted and snapped as tentacles sprouted from mounds of ruined corpses. Desiccated heads grew out of stomachs as horrible screeches and wails echoing. Claws oozed from anuses like putrid tar, a reminder that the damned had been reborn as new monstrosities.

Haley and Matt reached a hallway filled with the unearthly sight of a crawling horror. The thing was a hybrid of a woman and some unholy insect, its tentacles writhing, its chitinous limbs scuttling along the ceiling, emitting horrid clicks and screeches, and its claws tearing at the air.

On the floor, an obese man with silver hair lay in a copious puddle of blood, struggling for breath as some horrific monstrosity clutched him. It was humanoid, but a mass of squirming tentacles and black eyes with no whites eclipsed its body. The sight made their stomachs churn, and gag reflexes swell in their throats. Haley dragged Matt to a door, shoved it open with a bang, and they both darted inside. They slammed it shut behind them, securing it with a click.

Haley's voice was like a dry rasp, barely audible. "What kind of nightmare is this, Matt?"

A chill consumed them as they locked together in fear, not daring to move and witness the carnage that loomed in the shadows.

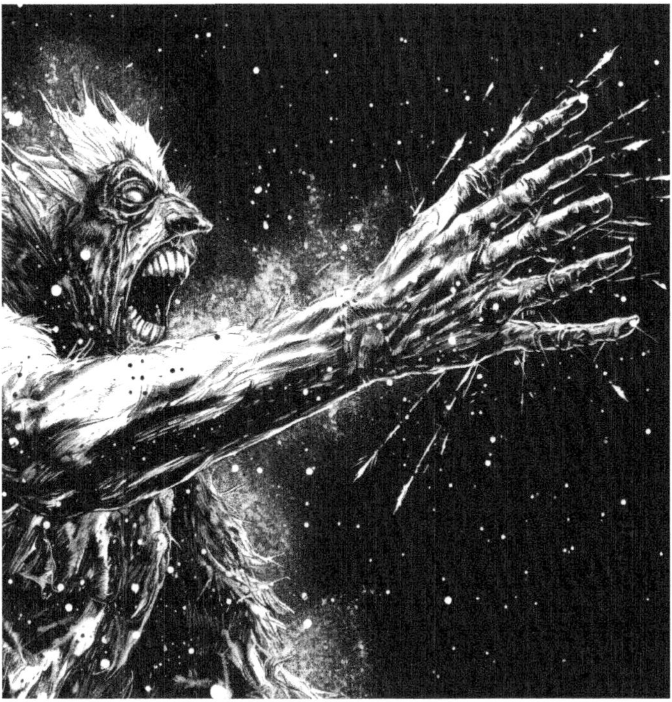

Feed Us

Chrissie's heart stopped when Matt and Haley vanished from her sight. The intruders on the dance floor showed no mercy. In a desperate prayer, she threw herself to the ground and hoped the creatures wouldn't spot her if she could still her trembling body. A silence surrounded her until she heard a faint clicking approaching. Her fear intensified when one of them, with its elongated tentacles, searched for life among the corpses scattered on the floor.

She dared to open her eyes a crack and saw the abominations of death before her. Corpses morphed and slithered on the ground, their howls reverberating off the walls in a cacophony of terror. Limbs from unknown creatures thrust through putrid flesh as grotesque shapes scurried about.

Piercing shrieks, squelches, and scrapes filled the room as though someone was mercilessly dragged across the floorboards. A guttural groan was the response to every violent crash.

She could hear the faint jingle of bells just above her head — the unmistakable decorations of Christmas Eve, which she had placed. A cloying, sickening smell suddenly filled the air, and Chrissie lay there immobile with fear, unable to move a single muscle. As it drew closer, she prepared to meet her death, praying that God would pity her and offer deliverance from this abomination.

She kept her eyes clenched tight as she felt the slithering tentacles of the creature run across her cheeks. Fetid breath wafted from its mouth as its scaly claws caressed her skin. As it loomed above her, a wave of terror swept her, and she was sure this was her last moment.

Chrissie then heard the blood-curdling toll of a gun and felt a rush of air as something — someone — galloped past her toward the exit. Petrified her in place, icy terror coursing through her veins, she opened her eyes cautiously, only to see the gym tarnished dramatically from its jubilant decoration. Seeing a detached leg lying beside her without its owner in view horrified her.

She skittered across the gore-soaked floor, her fingertips brushing against a warm puddle of viscera. The sounds of gunfire and agonized cries echoed off the walls, ringing her ears like a funeral bell. Praying silently for her children's protection, Chrissie left slug trails as she moved forward. As she infiltrated the exit, a bit of winter's breath blew in from outside, yet did nothing to soothe her terror.

She felt a presence behind her and spun around. There was her son. He was missing his left arm, and the rest of his body almost appeared to morph into some twisted abomination before her eyes. A clawed, scaly thing protruded from his back. It wriggled and snapped.

A loud gasp escaped her throat.

"Mike?"

She could hardly get out the name.

"Mom." His voice was a wet, strangled croak. "Thank God you're alive!"

The wet squelch of Mike's movements resonated through the room as he crawled across the floor. An ugly little reptilian face peeped out from beneath his neck. Chrissie felt a sudden emotion rush over her, and tears streamed down her cheeks.

"We have to get you out of here and to a hospital ..."

He inched closer until a rhythmic ticking filled the air. His body started to spasm and wriggle. His skin split open like an overripe fruit, revealing a mass of chitinous claws and lashing tentacles. Chrissie stumbled backward in terror, watching her son transform into something unspeakable.

"N-No!" she shrieked, her voice shaking with utter terror.

What had once been her son stood before her, unrecognizable now in its corruption. Its tentacles flailed wildly as it lumbered closer with each step, scraping the broken tiles beneath it.

The thing let out a guttural screech with a voice like gravel as it spoke. "Come closer, Mommy."

Uncontainable sobs erupted from her lungs, producing a strange, almost insectile sound. She froze in place, still shuddering and whining, "Not my baby, not my baby."

"Hug me Momma!" the ungodly abomination shrieked with an impossibly deep voice.

Its spindly tentacles twisted and clawed at her skin, drawing blood and tears. She fought to look away from the dismal creature that once had been her child, but was now unrecognizable in its mutated state. Rows of razor-sharp teeth lined its gaping maw and dripped saliva and putrid fluids onto her.

"Say it, Momma, say you love me!"

"No! Stop it!" Chrissie screamed, her tears like rivers of despair.

A monster, looming closer, had replaced her son, and there was nothing left of him. Its purulent feelers crawled around her body, caressing and touching, leaving a foul slime in their wake. Her mind shuddered at what had happened to her boy, consumed by the horrid, nightmarish creature she now faced.

"Feeeed ussssss!"

A cacophonous wail ripped through the air as it descended upon her, viciously tearing into her body. It ripped off her head and cast it aside in one swift motion. Her decapitated head landed on the floor with a loud thump, surrounded by an ever-expanding pool of crimson as it sprayed from her neck like a geyser.

Her body convulsed in a macabre dance, arms flailing, desperately trying to stop the blood flow from her severed neck. Then she crashed onto the floor like an invisible hand had jerked her legs from underneath her and lay there like a broken scarecrow.

With a clicking noise, the creature moved forward and ripped into its meal, consuming the blood pooling around its prey in a gory banquet.

A Run For Survival

At first, an unsettling and suffocating silence permeated the closet. Then, shrieking cries and pounding footsteps shattered the tranquility, drawing ever nearer. Haley grasped Matt's hand with a vise-like grip, terror snaking through their intertwined fingers. The presence of death was rapidly encircling them, trapping them with no hope of escape.

A loud boom shook the foundations of the building, and the floor seemed to lurch beneath them. Dread twisted in their guts as another crash followed — metallic and heavy — as if something were being pounded into submission. Then came a sound that made their hair stand on end: a sickening crackle and crunch of flesh against metal.

A trickle of blood seeped from beneath the door, growing wider each second until it pooled around their feet.

Inky blackness forced itself upon the room, broken only by a poisonous sliver of light entering through the slim opening in the threshold. Haley squirmed and clenched her teeth as a fiery pain thrummed deep in her calf muscle. She muffled her pained gasp with a pale arm and peered at Matt through white-rimmed eyes in pure terror.

"You alright?" Matt hissed in a panicked whisper, crouching inside the closet, determined to keep the beasts prowling outside from discovering their presence.

"Oh yeah, couldn't be better."

"Hey." He extended his hand and gently touched hers. "We'll make it out alive, I swear."

"This is so terrible," she whispered back.

With a trembling hand, she pulled out her phone and tapped it.

"Still no signal?" he inquired.

"Nope, nada. Whatever these bastards are, they've wiped out all power and communication."

"If we don't make it out of here alive ..." His words trailed off.

"Come on, bud," she said fiercely. " We're going to make it out of here. We can find our way out together."

The door creaked and groaned with an intensity that seemed to scrape the walls. A gurgled, distorted voice hissed through the keyhole, "Come out. I know you're in there. Should I get you? We are so hungry!"

Silence descended upon them like a shroud, the stark darkness intensifying their fear. Outside the door, a faint but unmistakable noise grew louder — something was scratching, searching for a way in. The door shook violently, and a voice rang: "We know you are in there!"

Matt grabbed Haley's shoulder and pointed up at the ceiling, at a rusted-out ventilation shaft, an escape route from the uncanny sounds outside the closet door. They both heard the slimy slither of tentacles, otherworldly clicks, and, worst of all, bone-splintering gurgles and human screams, as if something drained their life force.

Matt's stealthy movements prevented the metal grate from making a telltale sound. He plunged headfirst into the dank, winding passage, Haley following.

They heard a loud crash and wood splintering as they hurried down the musty-smelling shaft. An unsettling screech assailed their ears, and they knew the abomination had entered the closet.

The foul stench and annoying buzz of flies seemed to engulf them as they moved with ferocity — eyes squinted tight to flee the terror — heading for any faint glimmer of light that may offer deliverance.

They dropped to their hands and knees and crawled toward the basement boiler room. The darkness was absolute, and all around them was silence and fear, thick and oppressive like fog.

They sprinted through the bowels of madness, their fingertips frantically searching for purchase against walls of concrete and grime, only to find further hopelessness. The stench of death and pestilence assaulted their senses as something closed in from behind, a dark presence that echoed its malignancy through the blackness. The noise was ever-growing, relentless in its pursuit, and threatening to snatch them away at any second.

A jagged and unyielding object smashed against Haley's calf. She bit down on her bottom lip to contain the scream that was about to burst forth, lest the thing chasing them hear her.

Matt snatched her hand in his, his other hand blindly searching the dark. He clenched something hard and cold — a bar — and pushed it with all his might. A savage gale vented like a thousand icy blades ricocheting off their faces. The scene glowed an eerie blue, casting a sinisterly distorted portrait of them across a desolate loading dock. Nothing moved save for their labored breath, which cracked the stillness.

They rushed through the blizzard-ravaged parking lot, their soles smacking against the frozen layer of snow. Fear boiled within them as they hustled towards Matt's car, desperately trying to avoid whatever monsters lurked beyond the veil of white powder. The howling wind whipped, sending a flurry of powdery snow that ripped at their skin like tiny daggers. Terror propelled them forward as they desperately flew across the expanse, their hearts pounding in their ears.

Then they heard voices and saw bright lights piercing the snow-covered tree lines.

Making A Stand

Denise's car squealed as it careened along the icy road, her headlights and flashers illuminating the snow-glazed darkness. It was like an evil force that seemed to push against the car with an invisible hand. Streetlamps blinked out as she drove past them, until only an eerie, whistling wind remained. Denise was sure that if she went too far, she'd drive off the edge into a night from which there would be no return.

A siren-like howl ripped through the night, ringing in her ears. Her throbbing headache quickly became more intense as she fought to keep her focus on the dreary road ahead. Suddenly, the car sputtered and lurched to a stop. Frantically, she reached for her cell phone, only to find it had already died. She tried her walkie-talkie, but again, nothing — not even a flicker of life in its electronic systems. Panic rose within her.

She peered through the roiling storm, squinting at the silhouette of her destination. A quarter mile was all that remained between herself and the dance. Gritting her teeth against the chill, she hauled her shotgun from the backseat and trudged onwards into the white abyss, regretting with every icy step she had left her snow boots behind.

Through the bleak snow, Denise stumbled with her shotgun gripped tight. Her finger twitched on the trigger guard. The winter wind lashed like a whip at her frostbitten cheeks and nose. A deafening quiet surrounded her now, so loud it was easy to forget how lonely it felt. The presence of something beyond comprehension lingered in the shadows, always watching. Fear dug deep into her flesh like sharp claws.

"Christ Almighty!" Denise wailed, her voice shrill and quivering. Her eyes darted around the desolate expanse of snow-laden darkness, searching for answers that weren't there. She shivered against the loneliness and terror that coiled around her like a serpent.

A streak of fire cut through the night sky; its bright white light scattered across her every feature. She dove to the ground in the act of reflexive self-preservation. A powerful shockwave followed, sending up a plume of white.

"What the hell is that?" she cursed, trembling on all fours.

The pall of smoke billowed in the frigid air, a sign of whatever arcane catastrophe had just occurred. Her hands, even encased in thick woolen gloves, felt like lumps of lead as she pressed onward, the shotgun tight in her grip.

Her instincts screamed for her to flee, but some unknown force kept her going. Fearfully, she advanced, cautious of the shadows lurking in the night. Her senses tingled with an awareness of a presence nearby — something inhuman.

Her last conversation with her daughter had been about how excited she was to see Haley at the dance. Christmas was difficult for them, since her husband died on Christmas night three years ago. Denise's heart ached at the memory. The thought of losing her only child to some otherworldly creature made her feel like her heart was being ripped out.

As she approached, the screams grew louder. She felt naked and alone, not knowing what she was walking into. Holding the shotgun, she marched forward, ankle-deep in snow, toward the school.

A flood of paralyzing fear surged as she staggered forward, transfixed in terror. In the parking lot lurked a nightmarish beast — its wiry frame swathed in sapphire flesh, while its arcane claws and maw writhed with vicious tentacles that clutched an unfortunate soul in its deadly embrace. The victim squirmed feebly against the creature's oppressive clamp as innumerable spindly arachnids skittered about.

The winter snow cushioned her feet as she slowly raised the shotgun. She could feel her heart racing, but the cold air numbed her senses and seemed to still her trembling hands. All she could think of was seeing her daughter's face again. In this small town of Elview, where nothing ever happened — why did they have to be cursed with these monsters falling from the sky?

Denise moved with a feral intensity, the shotgun clutched in her hands.

Something materialized from the blizzard. It was a two-headed abomination, pulsing red and adorned with razor-sharp claws that gleamed cruelly. Like metal scraping against stone, a grinding noise invaded the air as it lumbered towards Denise with purpose.

Denise's gun erupted with a single resounding bang as the beast shot forward, jaws wide open. She seemed to dissolve instantly, in stark contrast to its tremendous size. Hot, thick blood cascaded onto the cold snow. The weapon crashed to the ground and fired one last round before becoming silent. A moment of stillness filled the air as the evil two-headed creature hovered over Denise's remains.

The creature's eyes darted around until they finally landed on Matt and Haley, who had come to a stop. Haley's scream of "MOM!" filled the air as she witnessed her mother's death.

The snowy night cast an eerie glow on the two human heads peeking out from the creature's stomach, their hollow eye sockets seeming to follow their every move. It approached them through the storm.

The Others Arrive

Matt confirmed his worst fears and felt his heart drop like dead weight — they would all perish here. A muted scream of terror erupted from behind Haley's quivering hands as she watched her mother perish before her eyes.

The split second felt like an eternity as options flashed through Matt's mind. One part was screaming to run back into the building, while the other was urging him and Haley to make a desperate dash for the car.

Another massive creature held onto a woman. She wore a red Christmas dress with white fur lining. It had pulled her skirt up, leaving her stomach exposed. Crouching over her, the creature ripped her open while burying its face in the gore.

Breaking through his terror, Matt turned to Haley, seeing her face locked in sheer disbelief. He bellowed, "LET'S GO!" as he seized her hand, and they sprinted towards his car, an eternity of agonizing seconds that passed like hours. The fear coursing through him caused Matt's manic thoughts to ricochet off the walls of his mind like a runaway train. The thing chasing them unleashed a hellish roar, causing snow to shoot into the air behind them.

Haley was sobbing as she ran.

He fumbled in his pocket for his keys, hoping he had left the car unlocked.

In a whirlwind of fear, Mr. Rollins, his former English teacher, rushed past him.

As Matt pushed Haley into the car, he felt an excruciating pain in his ankle, like fire trying to enter his skin. When he looked down, he found a tentacle coiled around his leg.

Matt tore away with every ounce of strength and hastily jumped behind the wheel.

"For fuck's sake, shut the fucking door!" Haley shrieked at him.

He slammed the door closed in one swift motion. An enormous tentacle smashed against it the next moment, rattling the entire vehicle. In an instant, a monstrous face pressed against the window, its obsidian eyes fixed on Matt. Just inches away from him.

The shadowy figure disappeared into a flurry of snowflakes, swallowed by the howling snowstorm. Matt watched it drift away until he couldn't see its silhouette anymore. He took a shuddering breath and tried to turn on the ignition, but all that answered him was a dull click.

He threw open the car door and stepped outside.

"What the hell are you doing?" Haley asked.

"Making a run for your mom's gun."

"No!" she screamed, tugging his arm. "They'll kill you too! There are too many of them."

Matt's foot had just fallen on the snowy ground when explosions lit up the night, bursts of orange light illuminating the horizon. It sounded like a war zone — thuds and machine gun fire thundering through the air. Matt and Haley locked eyes, overcome with fear. As quickly as lightning, they shut the door and hunkered underneath the windows, their hands clasped together in terror.

Matt and Haley froze in fear at the loud thump of knuckles on the glass. Peering out into the raging storm, they glimpsed a tall figure cloaked in camouflage, one hand clasping a gun fixed directly upon them.

"GET OUT!"

The blizzard howled like an avenging spirit, smothering the man's gruff voice, but even through the gale, the authority in his tone could not be mistaken. He waved towards the shadows, and from the darkness emerged a woman as dark as coal, wearing an arctic parka thick enough to survive an avalanche. Her handgun remained rigid at her side. He yanked open the car door, clamped each of them by the arm, and pulled them out. Pressing them onto their bellies, he placed handcuffs around their wrists. Gunshots crackled like thunderclaps throughout the white wasteland.

Haley whimpered, "Who are you?"

The woman answered, her tone matching the cold metal cuffs. "

We're from the CDC, and we're here to help. We must bring you to our research facility for examination. You have been exposed to something hazardous, and we must ensure you're not infected."

"Those things are everywhere!" Matt told them.

"We know," affirmed the man with sternness yet compassion. "Our crew is doing all they can to contain it, but our highest priority is keeping you safe and preventing contagion. Please believe us."

"I have no other option," Haley murmured in a quivering voice, her body trembling with despair.

YULETIDE INVASION

"Trust us," the woman said as she helped them stand up. "We'll get you out of here alive."

Haley nodded in agreement. Matt kept his gaze rigidly fixed on the blanket of snow beneath them, jaw clenched and teeth grinding, before finally relenting with silent acquiescence.

A truck charged out of the storm like a bull. A milky haze covered its windows, obscuring what was inside. The opening of the back doors filled Matt and Haley with gratitude and fear. With bated breath, Matt stepped inside, never taking his eyes off the strangers as he explored the ghastly interior for any signs of peril. Though they had survived, Matt knew this twisted nightmare could still devour them at any moment.

Gloria's blood ran cold, brought on by the awful memories from that fateful Christmas night long ago. Now, she and Emily stood face to face with the massive behemoths, their eyes black pits of despair. Emily let out a scream as spider-like creatures scurried around their ankles.

Gloria shouted, "This is just like before! Run for your life, and don't look back!".

With that, she grabbed Emily's arm, and they sprinted away, their heartbeats thumping like drums in time with their ever-increasing fear. They scrambled through the writhing mass of bodies, barely keeping upright as they made for the door.

The creatures were all over the place, extending their tentacles to grab anyone. People panicked and rushed to their cars, screaming.

Suddenly, there was a brush against Gloria's legs and she whirled around to see an abnormally tall, multi-legged beast. Its cacophonous clicking noise penetrated her ears like a barrage of tiny arrows. A tentacle brought her to her knees.

"You bastard!" she shouted. "Damn you to hell!"

The ground quaked and shook as an earsplitting boom ripped through the atmosphere. A brilliant orange light, akin to lightning, lit up the snow before them. In a single motion, Gloria lunged up, clutching Emily's hand as they fled from the commotion of gunfire and wails echoing in their ears.

"We got this. I made it out once before. Surely, I can do it again!" Gloria panted as they barreled through the snowscape towards the line of trees.

Another roar, louder than thunder, blasted down from above, and a blazing inferno descended straight on them, tumbling them in separate directions like rag dolls. Gloria's vision blurred and her ears buzzed as the blizzard-like conditions attempted to conceal Emily.

Gloria rose in defiance against the relentless snowfall that sought to devour her. She pondered how man had created a system of life so quickly taken for granted, then cried out in terror as an abomination lurched towards her, its putrid form a grotesque silhouette against the blistering backdrop of machine gun fire. Bullets ripped the abomination apart instantly, scattering bloody pieces like macabre confetti.

Out of nowhere, her broken body stopped obeying her commands.. A sudden agony ripped through her, paralyzing all attempts at movement. An explosion of light seared her vision, temporarily blinding her. Her spine curved in a sudden spasm and she fell unconscious, engulfed by nothingness.

Emily's Face

Gloria was suddenly back to her youth as she twirled around in a pale blue dress, a pattern of small flowers adorning it. Sam's broad grin sent shivers through her stomach as he stood beside her. The lake water lapped against her feet as they clasped hands beneath the hazy spray of the waterfall. The sun shone high in the sky, reflecting off the glassy lake surface surrounding them.

"You are a good friend to me, Gloria. Thank you," he murmured, his voice gentle.

Her lips curled into a reassuring smile. An intense wave of adrenaline rushed through her veins; the powerful sensation was almost tangible. She felt invincible like she had miraculously escaped an all-consuming storm. Despite the tumultuous events that life threw their way, Gloria knew they would endure it — united and undefeated.

She awoke with a start, her heart pounding like a sledgehammer in her chest and her skin prickling with anticipation.

Wavering shadows danced around her, embracing the oppressive darkness that threatened to consume her. A chill ran through her body like icy fingers clawing at her flesh while every bone ached, and her throat begged for water. The constant hum of an unseen presence filled her ears, growing louder with each passing second until it was deafening. Her mind raced and panic rose inside her like an unstoppable tide.

The air reeked of chemicals and death, the headiest fragrance being her fear. She pounded against the icy prison walls with all her strength, searching for any hint of escape. Suddenly, a single ray of light pierced through the darkness, offering a glimmer of hope. But as soon as it had come, it vanished, leaving her in cold emptiness again.

"HELP ME!" she bellowed, her voice reverberating off the walls with a haunting echo.

But there was no response — only an oppressive stillness and the ungodly hum swelling with each passing moment.

Where was she? What had brought her to this place? She had no recollection of how she even got here. Then it hit her — those alien bastards again, the explosions. Emily, her granddaughter ... where was she now? Was she here, too? The thought of Emily being here sent chills down her spine and intensified the anxiety building inside her.

"HELP!" she shrieked in desperation. Her voice was paper-thin and fraying as it echoed.

A glittering flash in the corner made Gloria jump as if struck with a bolt of electricity.

"Who's there?" she shouted, compelled to take baby steps toward the source of the flash.

"Shut your damn mouth!" a menacing voice hissed back. Her heart raced like an engine, searching the abyss for any trace of life and movement. "They'll come here and eat us alive if you keep talking, so shut up," the gruff voice added from within the darkness.

She searched the shadows for some sign of the speaker, her voice barely more than a whisper in her fear.

"Where are you? Who are you?"

"It doesn't matter. They have been picking us off one by one. Noises draw them like honey draws flies. Be careful, or they'll find you too."

The wheels in her head were turning faster than ever before. What was the purpose of this? Did they need people for food or some vile experiment? Or worse yet — were they to be used as vessels by which to propagate this cadre of monstrosities?

"They only took some of us away and left the rest down there."

She felt her stomach drop as his words sunk in.

"What do you mean by that? What's going on?" she anxiously cried out, fear clear.

"We're not home anymore. They have abducted us. You know what I'm talking about." His voice was low and severe.

Gloria's chest seized with fear, and her limbs trembled in the dark, cold air. She stumbled around, arms outstretched, calling for her granddaughter, "Emily! Are you here?!"

The only response was another brief shimmer of light. With every stride, Gloria's feet felt like dragging through the mud, and her eardrums thrummed to a constant low din. Yet another flash illuminated the bleakness, and she could faintly hear a clicking sound.

Then it came. Something moved in the dark, something barely audible but undeniably there.

"Who's there?"

Silence was her only answer.

Gloria smelled a putrid stench of decay and rot. Like drums pounding a war rhythm, thousands of clicking legs sounded nearer and nearer in her ears. Her heart raced, and her mind desperately searched for a reprieve from the nightmare that seemed to have no end. The wet, slithering noise got louder until it felt right upon her.

"Who is there?"

The clicking was now within inches of her ear. She could feel a warm breath on her neck in the pitch-black darkness surrounding her. Suddenly, there was another brilliant flash, and she saw it: a nameless, grotesque creature unlike anything she had ever seen before.

"Oh, my GOD!" she screamed.

The abomination before her began to stretch and contort. Out of its writhing mass, multiple faces emerged — faces of people she knew, including Emily's, trapped within some unknown horror.

She winced as the sensation of a thousand needles piercing her skin sent a searing pain through her body.

"NOOOOO!"

Gloria's last cry of despair accompanied her descent into the abyss. As she lay there, writhing in pain, she could feel the tendrils inside her twisting and grasping. She felt herself picked up and thrown onto her back.

The beast's many faces ripped into her with a ravenous hunger, and Emily's face was the last thing she glimpsed before everything went black.

Acknowledgements

A special thank you goes out to my incredible wife, Heather. She's the one who endures my incessant musings and questions that often teeter on the edge of the insanity. Her support, patience, and eagerness have been crucial to my success.

I want to thank my kids for the memories and fun that have fueled my drive for success.

I want to acknowledge the incredible work of my editor, Christine Morgan. Her attention to detail improved this book's less-than-stellar sections to make it the best for you all. She's not only a skilled editor but also a brilliant writer. I recommend checking out her book *"Lakehouse Infernal."* It kicks ass.

And I offer my heartfelt thanks to Matt Shaw, a beacon of wisdom and guidance through the darkest alleys of storytelling. Your advice has been invaluable on this creative journey, and I sincerely appreciate your help.

I am sincerely grateful to all of you who have supported my work. Your support fuels my creativity. Here's to the countless spine-tingling adventures and hair-raising horrors yet to be unveiled on the horizon.

I can't wait for our next journey into the world of horror.

J.C

Thank You

If you enjoyed this story, please leave a review on Amazon and Goodreads. I read them all, and they are appreciated. They help me grow as a writer.

LEAVE A REVIEW HERE

Get Free Stories

Although I may seem intimidating at first glance, give me a chance and you'll find that I'm a friendly guy. Most importantly, I enjoy connecting with amazing readers like you through my Cave of Horrors Newsletter.

Sign up to get free stories, musings, and cool recommendations.

jcmooreauthor.substack.com/

About the Author

J. C. Moore is an accomplished author, songwriter, father, husband, IT expert, and professional musician. He has worked as a bartender, owned a restaurant for a month, managed a horse farm, and toured the US with his band. Many television shows and movies have featured his music. He currently lives in upstate NY with his wife and his dog, Archie.

Printed in Great Britain
by Amazon